Contents

CW00972431

Chapter One
In the Park

'I'm telling you, blood...'

Devon leant over the smaller boy. Devon could see the nerve pulsing in the boy's forehead, see his eyes widening as they tried to look around, tried to find a way out. Devon smiled. These kids were so stupid, so scared!

'No one's here for you, you get me? Jus'

hand it all over.' Devon made his voice hard. Even though this kid wasn't going to give them any trouble, Devon felt the rush he felt every time.

Devon tightened his grip around the boy's wrist and felt the bones under the skin.

'Hear me now?'

'Let go! Let me go!' The boy's voice was high and girlish. The trousers of his new school uniform flapped over his shiny new school shoes.

'Give him the phone then!' Ash leant in towards the boy too, almost growling the command.

'I can't!' The boy squealed. 'He's got my hand.'

Devon shook the boy's hand away but stayed close. The boy fumbled in his pocket and a blue five pound note fluttered almost to the ground before Ash picked it up. The phone wasn't so great but the iPod that came out with it was a beauty. A woman passed with a pushchair, but she looked straight ahead and sped up. She was scared of them too, Devon could feel it. No one ignored Devon.

'No!' The boy was trying hard not to cry, Devon could see that, and he smiled down at him, waving the iPod in front of his face. He felt like he had the power to make anything happen.

'S'not yours anymore, see?'

Devon flicked a look at Ash and they jog-trotted away out of the park and past the astro turf into the estate. Then they sat down on the wall under Ash's balcony and laughed.

Chapter Two
At Home

Devon looked at himself in the mirror. The smart shirt was a bit too much but he had to admit he was looking good, even if it was only for his auntie's wedding reception. He had so many aunties he had argued that it didn't matter if he went or not. But Mum and Tamara, his sister, had been on his case nonstop big time about it.

Suddenly the door burst open and Tamara was there behind him in the mirror. She looked furious.

'Don't you know about knocking, sis?' Devon said, turning round. 'Dress looks good,' he added, smiling. 'You almost look as smart as me.'

'Don't chat rubbish to me, Dev. I'm your sister, not one of the Year Tens you like to love and leave.'

'Whassup? Mum found your cigarettes? Calm down, Tamara. I never wanted to go to this wedding either, but you don't see me making a fuss.'

'I have to talk to you.' She was speaking quietly. 'I don't want her to hear this, OK?'

Devon shrugged.

'This is serious, Devon!'

Tamara folded her arms and sighed. She looked straight at Devon one more time

and then went to look out of the window.
Devon's room had the best view; you could
see all of the city spread out below.

At last she spoke.

'I've heard some horrible things about
you. Really nasty things…'

Devon sat back on the bed.

'You shouldn't believe that crap going
around, people just like to hate, you get me?'

'Devon, you don't have to do that stupid
cool thing with me. I know you!'

'So what are they saying then? Surprise me.'

'Devon, I heard this from two people!
Two people I trust. Two different people
both saying the same thing. Both saying
that my little brother is stealing from little
kids! Twelve year olds, sometimes!'

Devon turned away and took out a
new pair of trainers from the bottom of
his wardrobe.

'And you believe them?'

Tamara looked at him.

'Do you think I am stupid or something? Do you think I don't notice how much spare money you have? That computer console, that phone!'

'Got it off this guy at school, yeah, and the phone was at Phoneshack, you know, in the high street. They do a good deal, serious.'

'Devon! I said, I am not an idiot.'

Devon turned away. Tamara went and sat down next to him on the bed.

'Dev, look, I have a job and I don't have that kind of phone.'

'Yeah, but you're just a hairdresser though. And I am telling the truth, Phoneshack does some good deals.'

'You're lucky Mum is too busy to nail you for this.'

'So you're gonna tell her?'

'She'd flip!' Tamara turned his face towards hers. 'She's got enough to deal with. She's working so hard just to keep everything going.'

'It's not me that's bothered about moving house.'

'She wants us to have a place of our own! Can't you understand that?' Tamara sighed.

'Devon, you can't keep doing what you're doing. You know what'll happen.'

Devon laughed.

'You should hear yourself, sis!'

'Don't laugh at me! You want to go to prison then?'

'No! I ain't going to prison, sis. It's nothing. You are so over the top, you know. Dramatic.'

'Don't you even think of those kids? The

ones you jack?'

'No! Why should I? And why should I listen to you? You work all day for what? A fiver an hour? Don't sound sensible to me!'

Tamara stood up. She was even angrier than when she had come in.

'Yeah well, you know what? At least I got a job! I don't see anyone anywhere ever employing you!'

Suddenly Mum put her head round the door.

'For God's sake don't tell me you two are arguing again! The taxi's here. Come on.'

Chapter Three
The Wedding

Devon looked down at his mum. They were standing outside the church hall waiting to go in. From inside the music was blaring and guests in their best suits and dresses poured in for the reception. Devon still wasn't used to towering over her, to looking down on to the top of her head. Mum reached up and smoothed his hair and he pulled away.

'Mum!' he said it quietly. Too many people might be looking.

'Worried someone will see?' She laughed. 'You're such a big boy now, looking so smart. I still wished you'd have let me buy you some nice shoes. Proper shoes.'

'These are brand new!'

'Trainers,' Mum shook her head. 'You know, I'm glad you came, Devon, we never go anywhere as a family. You and Tamara still angry with each other? I wish you'd be—' she sighed '—nicer to each other. What is it you two are fighting about now? Are there things you're not telling me, Devon? Do you want to talk to me?' Mum looked tired.

'No.' Devon looked away. He could see Tamara with her boyfriend Luke. They were talking with a younger girl, his age maybe, wearing a light-coloured, fitted dress that reached the floor.

'I'm sorry work's been a bit mad lately. You know what I'm doing though, Devon, it's for all of us. A place of our own.'

'Yeah, yeah.'

'I do worry about you. You have to go to school. Work hard. You used to get good grades y'know.'

'Mum! I'm not talking about this now!'

Mum sighed and took his arm and they walked into the hall. Devon was still looking at the girl. She had black hair in tiny plaits off her face, slanting eyes, and for a split second she looked straight back at him so fiercely Devon felt almost knocked off his feet.

'Is this your Devon?' One of Mum's friends had swooped on him and taken his head in her soft but strong old lady hands.

She smelled of talcum powder and she kissed him on the cheek.

'Andrea, your boy is grown up so handsome!'

Devon felt the blood rushing to his face. He looked up and saw the girl was watching, smiling.

It took Devon half an hour to get to the buffet. Every inch of the way some friend of Mum would come over and kiss him or hug him. They all said the same thing; variations on how much he'd grown and how smart he looked, and they all asked the same questions over and over, school, exams, college next year? Devon nodded and smiled and pretended he couldn't hear over the old-style reggae tunes the DJ was playing to keep the grannies happy.

He managed to get rid of Mum when she

saw her best friend Sonia waving from across the hall. Devon made for the buffet and helped himself to the chicken. There were a few people his age, but they were mostly younger; tiny ones running around under the tables in suits that didn't fit.

There were a couple of girls who were Tamara's old mates from school, but they did that 'Haven't you grown?' thing almost as well as the old ladies. He looked for the girl he'd seen outside but he couldn't spot her. She was worth looking for, beautiful and feisty. Not like Leann who had been chasing after him for months after they'd got off with each other at a party. And there was Danielle, a pretty face, good to be seen with, but she was so blank it was better not to talk to her.

Devon looked through the crowd again. Luke, Tamara's boyfriend, was making his way towards him. Luke was holding a paper plate full of chicken wings.

'Seat taken?'

Devon shook his head. Luke was all right most of the time, better than some of the boyfriends Tamara had had. But Devon could tell just by the way he smiled that Tamara had sent him over.

'All right Dev?' Luke said.

'You been talking to T?'

'Is it that obvious? Look, Dev, she is my girlfriend. I can't exactly not talk to her, and thing is, she is worried about you. Seriously.'

'Yeah, well maybe you shouldn't listen to what she says. She don't know everything you know, even though she acts like it most of the time.'

'True. It's big sisters. They're all the same.' Luke smiled. 'But still, take care

21

bruv, you need to be working hard, you know. Stick to the road.'

Luke took a bite of his chicken. Devon shook his head; he was as bad as Tamara sometimes.

'So who's the girl? The one with the plaits, nice eyes.'

Luke spluttered.

'Savannah? My cousin Savannah?'

'She's your cousin?'

'It's a small world, Dev, you should remember that. Everyone knows everyone, you get me? And yeah, Savannah's my cousin, my Aunty Marlene's girl.'

'I don't want a pedigree, man!'

'You're interested in Savannah?'

'I never said—'

'Oh-oh!' Luke put his plate down. 'She's a tough one, Savannah. Brainiac number one, no boys, too busy. Trains four nights a

week, not your kinda girl, from what T tells
me, that is.'

'I told you T don't know anything.
Trains? Trains at what?' Devon asked.

But Luke had been pulled out of his chair
by an old lady.

'Come now and dance with your granny,
Luke.'

And he was across the dance floor and
gone.

Devon smiled. Savannah. Nice name.

He put his plate down and made a
circuit of the hall, once clockwise, once
anticlockwise. Halfway round he found
Mum and Tamara, and Mum told him he
could go home if he was bored. But Devon
said no, he'd wait. After all he had
something to do now.

Eventually Devon spotted her by the
door, holding someone else's baby up to

look at the decorations.

'Savannah?' In his experience it was always best to take the direct route. She turned and smiled and the floor-length dress rippled. She was stunning.

'I don't know you, do I?' she said.

Devon thought her lips were beautiful. He would have liked to kiss her right away, but apart from the baby wriggling in her arms they were in a room full of people.

He put a hand out for her to shake. The corniest, stupidest thing he thought he had ever done. Savannah giggled and moved the baby so her hand was free, and Devon squeezed her hand and thought that maybe hand shaking wasn't such a bad move after all.

'It's not mine, you know—' their eyes met '—the baby.'

'No, I never thought—' Devon groaned

inside. He had hoped to keep the whole cool thing together. Now, still holding her hand, he had gone to pieces. Focus, he told himself.

'Are you OK? I mean, you're a bit flushed,' she said, looking concerned.

'No, I'm fine. I'm Devon.' He was falling on his face every time he opened his mouth. 'Devon. Tamara's sister? Luke's girlfriend, your cousin – I'm her, her brother.'

'Luke, yeah. Hi Devon.'

'Savannah! Have you got Nathan? Aah, Mummy's here.' A woman with a huge bright purple hat kissed the baby, but didn't pick him up.

'We're going now, Sav. Did you want a lift?' The woman looked from Savannah to Devon and back, then smiled. Now Savannah was blushing.

'Oops, was I interrupting?'

'Um, no, no, it's just— yes, I'll get my coat.' Savannah handed the baby over.

'Do you have to go?' Devon said.

Savannah made a face.

'I've got an early start. I'm training tomorrow first thing.'

'Training? Yeah, Luke said something about that. What do you do?' Devon looked at her. She was tiny, like a dancer, but they rehearse, he thought, they don't train.

'Circus,' she said as she left. 'I do trapeze. I'll catch you later,' she said, looking right at him with her almond-shaped eyes, 'Devon.'

Chapter Four
Phoneshack

Devon was sitting in the park with Ash
and he knew Ash was talking, but he was
thinking about Savannah. He had tried not
to all morning, and told himself if he
wanted a girl he should put Leann out of
her misery and go out with her again. He
was Devon Read. He was in control. Kids
handed over their money, girls fell at his

feet. Why wouldn't Savannah? Devon smiled. He just had to find out where she lived or went to school. Failing that how many places where you could go and do trapeze? And was that really what she had said? Trapeze. He thought of Savannah in one of them all-in-one things, leotard, that was it…

Ash took the iPod out of his jacket pocket and scrolled through the list of tracks.

'You're not listening, Dev, are you?' he said suddenly.

'Oh, what? Yeah, sure.'

'See. I've put in those tracks off of Steve's now, if you'll just let me download the ones you got.'

'Yeah anytime, Ash, anytime.'

'I got to go in to speak to some student adviser about something,' Ash said, looking up. 'Options after sixteen. I said I don't mind going to college. My brother did Sports Science, he said it was better than school.'

'Anything's better than school,' Devon agreed. 'And that's why I'm not there!'

'Laters Dev. You coming up Phoneshack with me and Steve, yeah?'

'I'll be there, Ash.'

Devon watched Ash as he walked away. The park was just full of mothers and babies and old people feeding the pigeons. If he didn't move on, one of them would have a go about him not being in school.

All that bothered him was how would he find out about Savannah? Devon walked out of the park and towards the Narroway where there was a good chippy. He passed the library where he could see banks of computers through the glass and the words: FREE INTERNET ACCESS.

Half an hour later he had the address of the Circus School. He'd just typed the two words in and there it was, only a ten minute bus ride away. London Youth Circus was on tonight – it had to be the same one. He could check it later, after he'd met up with Ash and Steve.

Phoneshack was on the Narroway in between a curtain shop and a burger place.

Carl, who worked there, was always happy to advance some money on future earnings. The shop repaired and sold phones and there were always people hanging around waiting to hook up with Carl or Raj. The counter was at the back and shoulder high, and grubby glass cabinets offered a selection of second hand phones and MP3 players. CASH ONLY was written on a poster behind the counter.

'So boys, what you got?' Carl was busy writing a message on the blackberry in front of him on the counter.

'Not much just now,' Devon said, taking the phone out of his bag. 'Found this over in the park, last week.' It was the one they'd taken off the schoolboy.

Carl barely looked at it.

'No use to me,' he said.

Ash kissed his teeth.

'It's new, though!'

Carl put down his blackberry.

'I can only get twenty for one like that, new or not. I need something else.'

The boys looked at him.

'Couldn't you forward something?' Ash said.

'Like, on account?' Devon asked.

'Things are tight right now, boys. This ain't no student bank!' Carl had picked up his blackberry again.

Devon looked at Ash and Steve and they started walking out of the shop. Devon knew Carl well enough to know there was no arguing with him.

'I need some cash, man,' Devon said. He looked at his watch. It was six. He needed to get down to the Circus School and see Savannah.

When they got to the park it was emptying out. Even the ones who stayed late at school for orchestra were gone.

'They'll all be eating their tea in front of *Hollyoaks* by now,' Steven said, looking out across the swings.

'We could try the older guys, wait out near the station,' Ash said. 'Intercept them on their way home.'

'Intercept! Have you been watching *University Challenge?*' Devon said. 'I can't stay. I need to be gone. Catch you laters, yeah.'

'You got course work or something?' Ash said, smiling.

'Yeah, right!' Devon said. 'Nah, man, something much sweeter.'

Devon spent half an hour choosing the right basketball top. Tamara didn't get in until after six and there was a message on the answerphone from Mum saying she had a meeting so he could take his time. He found a tenner in Tamara's room and got the bus to the Circus school. Then if Savannah was up for going out straight away – and she had been interested, he was sure of it – wasn't he? Devon caught his reflection in the bus window. Yeah, he was sure.

Chapter Five
Savannah

Devon was relieved there was no one round
he knew to watch him. He waited outside
the circus school building imagining
Savannah just walking out and him
catching her, 'by accident', on her way
home. After twenty minutes he couldn't
wait any longer. He took a deep breath and
walked past the heavy doors twice before he

finally pushed them open.

Inside there was a café, tables and chairs and huge glass windows on to a high-ceilinged hall. In the hall Devon could see a run of mats on to a trampoline, and a line of girls and boys taking turns to run and flip. None of them was Savannah. Maybe he'd got the wrong night. He looked up. In the roof of the hall there was what looked like a giant swing, and a tiny girl swinging backwards and forwards, then almost falling and grabbing the bar with her hands and somersaulting around. Devon's jaw almost hit the floor. It was Savannah. She looked fearless. She had a safety belt, but there was no net and she was at least four meters up.

'Yeah, she's good isn't she?' There was a girl behind the bar wiping the counter with one hand and watching Savannah.

'Um, yeah, suppose so. Can I wait?'

'Be my guest.'

Devon watched. Savannah swung and hung by her feet, by one arm, by her knees. He watched as she slid down a rope effortlessly to the ground.

He watched her unclip her safety belt and take a drink from the water fountain. Then, as she stood up, she saw him and waved.

In two seconds she was walking towards him, talking through the glass. Her skin shone brown like dark honey.

'Five minutes.' She mouthed at him through the glass.

'Five minutes.' Devon mouthed back. He thought he would have waited hours if she asked.

'I don't know how you do that.' Devon was smiling at her as they sat in the café.

'It's the feeling,' Savannah said. 'The air rushing past and just – I can't explain, it's that feeling when you know you can do something. You just feel so, so alive I suppose. God, I bet I sound stupid!'

Savannah untied her plaits, which were pulled back into a pony tail, and shook them free.

Ask her now, Devon told himself.

'So is there any time you don't train? Weekends maybe?'

'Are you asking me out?'

'Might be,' Devon said.

'We're doing a show here next month. You should come.'

'Circus ain't my thing, babe. Really though.'

'This isn't clowns with red noses stuff, Devon. This is different. You should come.'

Devon looked straight into her eyes and

she didn't look away.

'Are you asking *me* out?' Devon said smiling.

The next day Devon still felt like he was walking on air. He was nice to Mum before she went to work and washed up the breakfast things and didn't shout at Tamara.

Ash and Steve were grinning too as he saw them sitting on their bench in the park.

'We hit gold last night after you left, Dev,' Ash said.

'Yeah. A laptop, one of them Sony ones,' Steve went on. 'It was outside that station by the park. This guy comes off the train and there's no one else around and we just swooped.'

'Like death from above!'

'Only we never killed him though.'

'No, just scared him shitless.'

'Yeah!'

Devon felt himself back to earth in seconds. He'd been remembering walking Savannah home, and the way she smiled at him, and the promise of the weekend.

'What? You got a laptop? For real?'

'Shh, man! Yeah. Carl is going to be handing over those notes.'

'You should have been there,' Steve said. 'Seen the look on the guy's face. What a mug!'

Devon said nothing. If he had some more money he could buy something for Savannah, show her how he felt. They could go up the West End.

'Dev, come on,' Ash clapped him on the shoulder. 'If we're there tonight, you can get some for yourself.'

Devon said nothing. He was texting Savannah.

'S. Thinking of you, Dx,' it read. Ash pulled the phone out of his hand.

'S? Who's S then?'

'No one you know,' Devon said.

'Is it that Simone Gallagher in Prospero Tower?'

'No! You don't know her. She goes to Sir Henry Arden.'

'Them girls are posh, man!' Ash said. 'Does she know all about you yet?'

'Obviously not,' Steven said.

'Shut up!' Devon took his phone back. He remembered Tamara shouting at him in his bedroom. *Jacking little kids.* Put it like that and it sounded really low, even if the kids they took things off deserved it. They all had insurance and anyway their mummies and daddies probably just went right out and bought them newer phones. I mean, the stuff some kids had in their pockets.

If you looked at it like that, Devon thought, he was doing those kids a favour, but Savannah wouldn't see it like that. And what if Tamara said something to her about him? Or Luke? What would she think of him?

Devon tried to shut those thoughts off. Savannah liked him, she'd said so, they'd agreed to meet again. Devon looked at Ash and Steve. He thought about them, walking down the corridor like they owned it, the younger kids getting out of their way, not daring to look at them. He knew that feeling, he liked that feeling, but did he like Savannah more?

After school Devon went to Phoneshack again with Ash and Steve, and Carl gave them one hundred for the laptop. It was the most money he'd ever paid them for anything and Devon couldn't help feeling a little bit jealous that he hadn't been part of it.

They walked back past the station and there was a yellow police notice board with yesterday's date. ASSAULT it said in black letters. Ash and Steve stood either side and Devon took their photo on his phone. They were joking and laughing and doing gangster poses.

'You lot in big trouble now!' Devon said it lightly, but he thought Tamara would kill him if the police picked him up, let alone what his mum might do – if she was ever home from work long enough to notice, that is.

Ash kissed his teeth.

'It wasn't serious, man!'

'We never touched him,' Steven said.

'So how did you get him to hand over the laptop then? You just asked very nice and polite?' Devon said. 'I don't think so.'

Ash smiled and put his hand inside his jacket and pulled out a short-handled knife with a shiny blade.

'This. Should have seen the guy's face!'

'You said that already,' Devon said. 'You told me about how the man's a mug, about how scared he was and about the stuff you found on his computer, I dunno, ten times, twenty times? You got nothing else to say?'

'Is our conversation boring you, sir? Yeah, well you'd do the same if you were fifty notes richer.'

They walked back to the park and took their usual place on the bench, but Devon was twitchy. What if Savannah saw him now? Or Luke, or someone who'd tell Savannah her new guy was doing what he was doing...

'What's up with you, Dev? It's like you

got ants up your boxers!'

'Nah, man. I dunno, I just—'

'You don't need any cash? You got a money tree at home or something?'

'I'm going, all right.'

Devon walked away. He didn't look back. He couldn't start to think what Ash or Steve, whom he'd known since Year Seven, would be thinking. He took the phone out of his pocket and thought he might go up the Circus School again and catch Savannah, but checked himself; she might think that was a little creepy.

Instead Devon turned for home.

Chapter Six
The New Man

Devon walked Savannah home along the
canal. It was the second real date they'd
had and it had been a good choice of film.
One of those really scary ones that had
made Savannah jump and hide her face up
against him. Devon stopped by the lock
and kissed her again. Savannah laughed
and ran away, balancing along the edge of

the lock gates. Now it was Devon who couldn't look.

'Savannah, get down! You'll fall!'

Savannah walked nimbly across to the other side.

'I won't, you know. Come and get me! Or are you chicken?'

'No!'

'You are! All right, chicken boy!' She had started back before he could say anything. 'You never did low or high wire so I suppose it is different for you.' She took his hand and kissed him. Devon thought that if anyone had ever called him any kind of name like that before he'd have floored them.

'I wasn't scared OK? Circus girl.'

Savannah laughed.

'I guess I like a bit of danger.'

'That's why you like me, is it? Dangerous Devon? I'm not really dangerous no more, you know. You tamed me proper.' She didn't know how true that was. He'd even been to school for a whole week.

'I told Luke, my cousin, you know, he warned me off. He told me you were a bad boy. But I said you weren't like that.'

'Really? I thought you said you liked danger?'

'Like on the trapeze I mean, I like a buzz.' Savannah shrugged. 'I don't want my life to just be watching TV, seeing what Beyoncé is wearing, that kind of thing. When I go to Uni—'

'You're going to Uni?'

'Course, Dad says I should be a lawyer – I dunno about that, but I don't want to be working in a shop my whole life.'

Devon went quiet. He should have said something else. Of course a girl like Savannah was going to University.

'Luke said something else about you…'

'What did he say?' Devon tried to sound calm but his heart was pounding.

'He said you were a bully. But I knew you couldn't be.'

'You want to meet a bully you should see my sister. She's hard!'

'Tamara? Sounds good to me, I'm a big sister myself.'

'You telling me you got even prettier sisters?'

'No, stupid! Brothers, three of them, little ones: Jamal, Jayden and Jerome, and I am so hard on them. For their own good, you understand. I expect that's what Tamara's doing. Keeping you in line until I can take over.'

'So you're saying you're taking me over then?'

Savannah took his hand and looked deep

into his eyes. Devon felt his heart speeding
up so fast he thought it would burst.

'Looks like it,' she said and kissed him.

They walked back to her house on the new
yellow brick estate. Savannah opened the
door; the hall was full of bikes and shoes.

'Six people in one small house.' She
shook her head. 'I am so looking forward to
leaving home!'

Devon smiled. He could hear the
computer game going in the front room
and from upstairs someone was playing
music. The house felt so different from his
own quiet flat.

Savannah put her head round the door of
the front room and pointed at the two boys.

'Jamal and Jayden.'

Devon said hello and smiled. The two
boys kept their eyes glued on the racing
game on screen.

'My brothers are so rude.'

'Give them some slack! They're busy,
I can see that!'

'Where's Jerome?' Savannah asked them.
'Shouldn't he be home by now?'

'Oh, he just called.' One of the boys
turned round. 'His mate Reece got jacked
at the bus stop. The police are giving them
a ride seeing if they can see the guys who
done it. We told Mum and she went to
meet them. 'S OK Sav, no one's hurt.'

Savannah took Devon into the kitchen.

'Are you all right, Dev?'

Devon nodded.

Savannah carried on talking.

'I hate it when people do that, they're
just kids. It is beyond sick.'

Devon looked out into the small
garden and felt his insides turn over.
Savannah was ranting and her words

just sort of melted together.

'Low lifes, thugs, robbing eleven year olds!'

'Savannah, cool down. They're OK, nobody's brains dash out!'

'It's not just that!'

'And Savannah, that kid's probably gonna get a new phone or gameboy or whatever. So there's no harm to it!'

Savannah stopped what she was doing and stared at him.

'I cannot believe you just said that!'

'What?'

'Maybe Luke was right.'

They looked at each other saying nothing. Devon waited for her to apologise, to hug him and say never mind, but she didn't. He stood up and walked out of her house, slamming the door on the way.

Chapter Seven
Too Good to be True

'Haven't seen you around much, Dev,' Ash
said outside school.

'I been at school.'

'Full time? You're jokin' me.'

Devon said nothing.

'It's that girl, I bet, yeah,' Ash said. 'She
putting you under manners? You a good
boy now?'

Devon looked away. Savannah wasn't returning his calls and it made him feel sick thinking about it.

'So how's business?'

'Good, good. Carl is coming across with the notes now. See my new phone?'

Ash flipped a shiny clamshell black model out of his pocket.

'Does everything, video an' all. You should hang with me and Steve. We have missed you, bruv.'

''S cool.'

'You turning into a mamma's boy?'

'No!' Devon was smiling but he turned away in case Ash could see his face.

'You lie! You're different now. I seen it just now coming out of school, no one gets out of your way so quick these days, Dev, you're losing it.'

Devon looked back at him hard.

'That is so not true, bruv.'

'So show me. Come over the park with me now. Steve's waiting, or won't the missus let you?'

'She is nothing, you get me.' Even as he said it Devon knew he was lying. He still thought about her all the time.

They walked past the school and the bus stop and across the park. Devon said nothing but inside he felt torn. He knew what Ash was saying was true. He had been trying to stay clean and then call Savannah, tell her he wasn't like any of that and it would all be worth it. He took out his phone as they walked and dialled.

'There's so many stupid kids around, Dev. It's mad not to teach them some lessons.'

'I thought you were after the older age group these days.' He flicked a look at his phone. She hadn't answered.

Ash shrugged.

'If and when, Devon, if and when. There's more heat off doing an old man. The police and that all want to get involved. You take stuff off these kids, there's no come back, none at all. It's like fruit off the trees.'

'You getting poetic, Ash?' Devon said. Inside he was willing Savannah to pick up.

Steven was waiting, sitting on the back of the bench, feet on the seat. Smoking a cigarette.

'The boy returns!' he said, seeing Devon.

Devon shook his head and checked his phone. It stopped ringing. He put it to his ear. 'This is the voicemail…' Devon clicked it off. She had her chance.

Suddenly Ash nudged him. Two boys, one small, one tall, but spindly – Year Nines probably – were coming towards them. They had navy blazers, which meant they could only be Sir Henry Arden. Savannah's school.

Steve got up and flipped up his hood. Devon could feel the rush, the excitement as the two boys got nearer, seeing them pretending not to be scared, tensing up, looking around for a way out, for someone to help. Devon stood up too. So what if it got back to her? He could feel the buzz again. Savannah didn't know what she was talking about.

Ash waited until they were level.

'Got the time?' Ash kept his voice low and the smaller boy looked up. Devon realised instantly it was Jamal. But it was too late now.

The boys said nothing and would have walked on, but Steve blocked their way.

'I need to know,' Steven said. And Devon could see the big guy getting flustered. He was never Year Nine, Year Eight but big.

'Just hand it over,' Devon said. If they got this over quick it would be better. He gripped the front collar of tall boy's blazer. He couldn't look at Jamal.

The tall boy handed over a phone and one of those crap no brand MP3 players. Ash kissed his teeth and turned to the smaller kid just as Devon let the big one go. There was a look between the two Sir Henry boys and the small one kicked Ash hard in the groin and they both ran, shouting, towards the swings.

Steve went after them immediately and Devon stood frozen, wanting to let them go. Ash was furious, doubled over in pain. Then Steve shouted, 'Come on!', and they followed, Ash at half speed, swearing and spitting, until the pain had gone enough for him to straighten up.

The two boys legged it over the fence at the far side of the swings and across the road. A car nearly knocked into Steve but he missed it, and Devon almost caught up with him on the far side.

'They've gone in the station!' Ash said, still running.

Devon and Ash ran in after them up the stairs. The platform was long and empty. No one used the station in between the rush hours and there was never anyone in the ticket office or up on the platform.

'Which one?' There were two sets of stairs, one to each platform. Devon, Ash and Steve stood in the ticket office, out of breath.

'Let's leave them, come on. We'll get

them another time. All right?' Devon
thought he could talk the others away. Get
them to leave the kids alone. He'd tell
Savannah it had been a joke, they were
just winding the little kids up, that's all.

'That midget's not getting away.' Ash
took out the knife that was in his pocket.
Devon felt his blood chill.

'Forget it, Ash, they're probably shitting
themselves just knowing we're down here!'

'I'm going up this one. Steve you take
the other.' He turned to Devon. 'If you
want to be a pussy just go home now. I'm
only gonna scare them.'

Devon followed Ash up the stairs to the
platform. Maybe he could still stop it. He
walked up the steps, his feet like lumps of
lead. He had to stop it. But Ash wouldn't
use it, would he?

The platform was up high at rooftop

level, and the wind blew hard across the huge expanse of flat grey concrete.

There was one woman with a pushchair in the shelter, who flinched when she saw Ash and Devon. Devon saw her eyes flick down to the knife in Ash's hand and she pulled her pushchair closer.

Steven came up on the platform opposite and shook his head. He hadn't found them. Devon felt the relief wash over him. It would be OK.

He touched Ash's arm.

'Let's go, man.'

Suddenly there was a noise on Steven's platform. Devon and Ash looked across and saw a black trouser leg from behind the shelter on the other platform.

Devon tensed. Ash motioned to Steve who grabbed one boy, the tall one, while the little one bashed Steven with his bag shouting, 'Let him go!'

That was Jamal, no question about it.

Suddenly Ash vaulted down on to the track and across to the other side, knife in hand.

'Ash, wait!' he shouted, and ran across after him. Devon knew he had to stop him; he vaulted up on to the platform just in time to see the Sir Henry's boys scatter. One tried to make the staircase dodging Steven, the other jumped down on to the track.

The woman with the pushchair was screaming something and Devon looked round and one of the airport express trains that don't stop until they reach the city powered through and drowned out her words.

Chapter Eight
Afterwards

The police came in seconds. The air ambulance came as well but it was too late for the boy, and Devon heard the paramedics say his name. *Jamal.* He was dead.

And Devon tried to explain to the police, it was an accident, no way was Ash really going to hurt anyone, even if it looked that way. And that witness, that woman, hadn't seen the smaller boy kick Ash in the park, so hard he was bent double.

'It was an accident.' Devon said it over and over, to the duty lawyer and the woman from social services and Tamara and eventually, his mum, and he hoped that, if he said it enough then he would believe it and it would be true.

And he knew Savannah never would.